Baby Ca

By P. Mignon Hinds
Illustrated by James Needham

A GOLDEN BOOK • NEW YORK
Western Publishing Company, Inc., Racine, Wisconsin 53404

Text © 1988 Angel Entertainment, Inc. Illustrations © 1988 James Needham. All rights reserved. First published by Longmeadow Press.
Printed in the U.S.A. No part of this book may be reproduced or copied in any form without written permission from the publisher. GOLDEN,
GOLDEN & DESIGN, GOLDENCRAFT, A GOLDEN BOOK, A GOLDEN LOOK-LOOK BOOK, and A GOLDEN LOOK-LOOK BOOK & DESIGN
are trademarks of Western Publishing Company, Inc. Library of Congress Catalog Card Number: 90-81294   ISBN: 0-307-12605-6/
ISBN: 0-307-62605-9 (lib. bdg.)   MCMXCII

On a warm summer afternoon, Mother Cow gently licks her newborn calf clean. Baby Calf has beautiful dark eyes. He cannot see very well now. But soon he will be able to see the world more clearly.

Before long, Baby Calf feels strong enough to stand. Since he is just a few hours old, his little legs are very wobbly. He tries again and again, but he keeps falling!

At last, Baby Calf stands for the first time. He is trying so hard that he does not even notice a beautiful orange-and-black butterfly fluttering nearby. It lands right on top of Baby Calf's forehead.

A young cow approaches Baby Calf and makes a quiet mooing sound. It is his older sister. The one-year-old heifer has come to meet her new brother. She touches her nose to his in a gentle greeting.

Suddenly, the farmer's dog rushes toward the pasture fence, barking loudly. Mother Cow does not know that he is only playing. She quickly moves to protect her baby from any harm, and the frisky dog dashes away.

Baby Calf is hungry. He nuzzles against his mother's big, warm belly. Mother Cow has plenty of fresh milk for Baby Calf to drink.

While Baby Calf is nursing, the farmer's son leads the other cows into the barn to be milked. Since Mother Cow is nursing her baby, she will not be milked today.

Inside the barn, machines gently milk the cows. Dairy cows produce many gallons of milk every day. Because they produce so much, they feel very full until after they have been milked.

After milking, the cows return to the pasture. By mistake, one cow steps on a nest of yellow jackets. The insects fly out of their nest, and buzz all around the herd. The cows simply wave their tails to shoo the yellow jackets away.

While the cows graze on grass and yellow clover, a squirrel scampers through the pasture fence. The little animal runs up a nearby tree. It perches on a branch overlooking the pasture, and looks Baby Calf right in the eye.

The sun is slowly disappearing from the summer sky.
Mother Cow settles down for the night on a bed of
straw. Baby Calf lies down next to his mother. Soon
both will be fast asleep.

Facts About Baby Calf (A Guernsey Cow)

Where Do Cows Live?

Cows feel at home on open pastures, where they roam and graze within large fenced-in areas. Some cows live in barns that have stalls with straw floors. Cows can adapt to both hot and cold climates. Guernsey cows are raised on dairy farms in almost every state, as well as in Canada. This breed is one of the biggest milk producers on American farms.

What Do Cows Eat?

Cows are vegetarians with big appetites. A calf is usually five to ten weeks old when it begins to eat farm food. Dairy cows eat lots of grass and hay. They are also fed silage, which is a mixture of clover, oats, corn and alfalfa. To produce large amounts of milk, dairy cows must drink plenty of water. Cows can eat without chewing because their stomachs have four parts. They store food, then bring it up later to chew and swallow.

How Do Cows Communicate?

Mooing sounds are heard throughout pastures as cows spend lazy days in their herds. Cows also communicate with their huge bodies. These gentle animals use body movements to show affection or warn others of danger. To protect her calf, an angry mother might lower her head to charge. Since cows are not very smart animals, they often do not learn to respond to being called.

How Big Are Cows, and How Long Do They Live?

Guernsey calves weigh about one hundred pounds at birth. They grow to be as heavy as eleven hundred to seventeen hundred pounds. Adults are about five feet tall. Most dairy cows produce milk for about six years, but they can live twenty years or more. Farmers usually only keep cows that are giving milk.

What Is A Cow's Family Life Like?

Many young heifers are mated at about one and a half to two and a half years old. After nine months, one or two babies are born. Farmers sometimes start to feed baby calves with bottled milk after they are just a few days old. Other farmers let calves nurse on their mothers' milk for a longer time.

What Are Cows Raised For?

Dairy cows are very important farm animals. They supply milk for us to drink and butterfat to make butter. Milk is used to make cream, cheese and ice cream. Each dairy cow produces many thousands of pounds of milk each year. Only female cows give milk. Cows also provide meat for people to eat, including beef and veal. Other products made from cows are leather, medicines, soap and glue.